Saviour Pirotta has always been fascinated by colour. Before moving to the UK he grew up on the island of Malta, where the main colours were the yellow of the sun and the blue of the Mediterranean sea. Today he lives in Yorkshire, where everywhere seems to be a cool green. Saviour has a large collection of basketball shoes, all different colours. He likes matching them with his glasses. His current favourites are a bright red, which also match the colour of his favourite food, watermelon. Saviour has also written *Joy to the World*, *Little Bird* and *Turtle Bay* for Frances Lincoln.

Linzi West lives in a very old red house by the green sea in Lyme Regis, Dorset. On grey days she works in her [illegible] er black and white cat with the pink nose, called Pebble. On sunny [illegible] puts on her orange hat and brown coat to walk on the yellow sand under blue skies dreaming up amazing colourful pictures for her new books. Linzi is the illustrator of the *Cat* and *Dog* board books by Jane Kemp and Clare Walters and she has also written and illustrated *A Beach Ball Has Them All* and *Warm Sun, Soft Sand*, for Frances Lincoln.

For Giovanni Currah – S.P.

For Joseph – L.W.

First published in Great Britain in 2007
by Frances Lincoln Children's Books, 4 Torriano Mews,
Torriano Avenue, London NW5 2RZ

www.franceslincoln.com

First paperback edition 2008

British Library Cataloguing in Publication Data
available on request

ISBN 978-1-84507-719-8

The illustrations in this book are pastels

Printed in Singapore

1 3 5 7 9 8 6 4 2

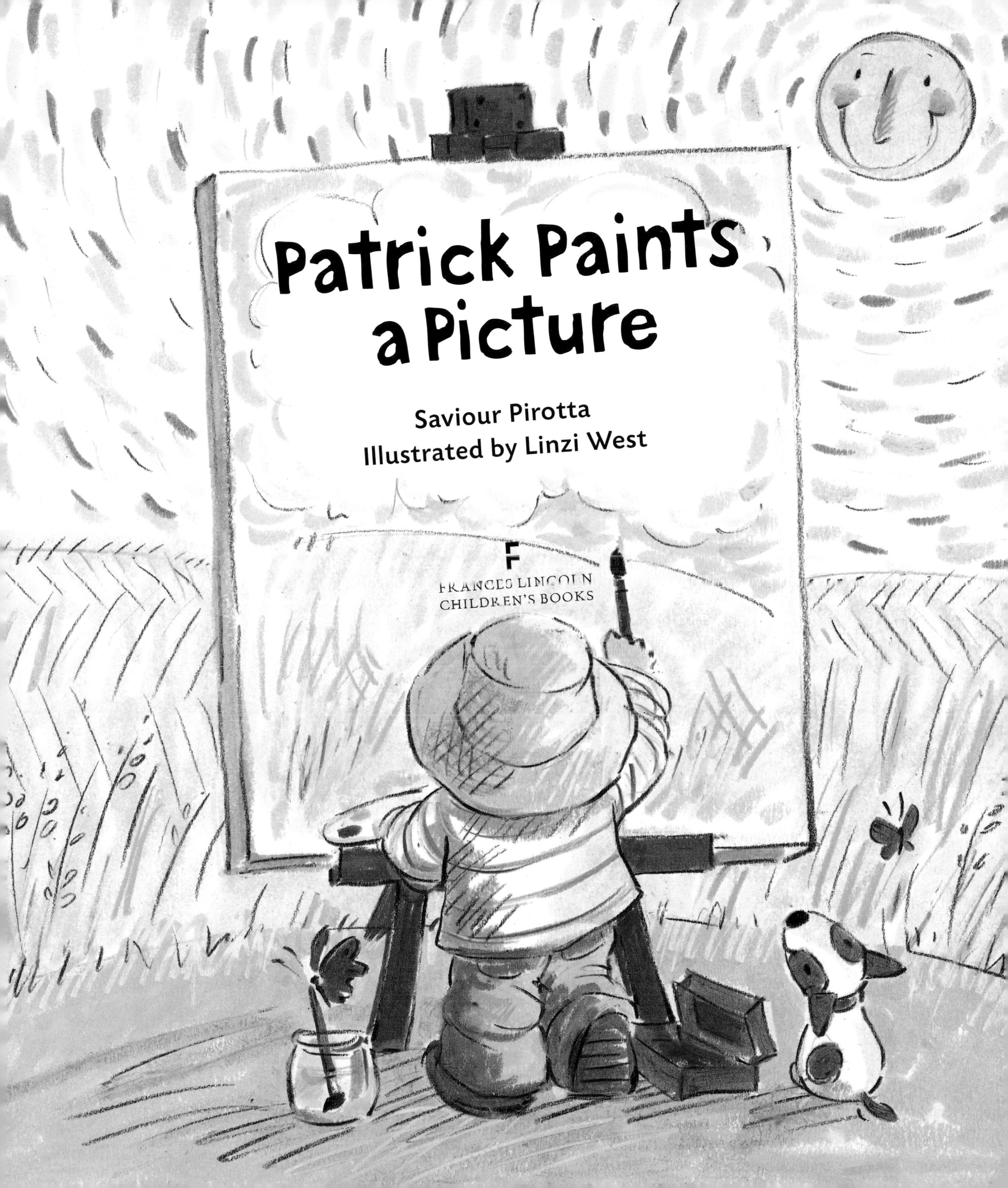

Patrick Paints a Picture

Saviour Pirotta
Illustrated by Linzi West

F
FRANCES LINCOLN
CHILDREN'S BOOKS

Patrick and Aunt Emily were sitting in the shade of a tree. "Let's paint a picture of that cornfield," said Aunt Emily.

They looked at the corn swaying in the breeze.
"What colours do we need?" she asked.

"YELLOW," said Patrick.

"That's right," said Aunt Emily.

A squirrel appeared in the corn, hunting for nuts.
"Now we need yellow and..."

"RED," said Patrick.

"Red for a red squirrel," said Aunt Emily.

A bird settled on the ground, peck-peck-pecking around for bits of straw. He was building a nest.
"Now we need yellow, red and..."

“**BLUE**,” said Patrick.

“Blue for a bluebird,” agreed Aunt Emily.

A butterfly danced round and round
in the air, enjoying the warm sunshine.
"Now we need yellow, red, blue and..."

"PURPLE," said Patrick.

"Right again," said Aunt Emily.
She showed Patrick how to make purple
by mixing blue and red.

In the cornfield, a frog hopped out of the shade.
“Now we need yellow, red, blue, purple and...”

"GREEN," said Patrick.

"That's right," said Aunt Emily.
She showed him how to make green
by mixing blue and yellow.

Baa! A lamb skipped into the field, calling out for its mummy.
"Now we need yellow, red, blue, purple, green and..."

"WHITE," said Patrick.

"I like white," said Aunt Emily.

Oink! Oink! A piglet followed the lamb into the field, sniffing around for some wet mud to roll in. "Now we need yellow, red, blue, purple, green, white and..."

"PINK," said Patrick.
Aunt Emily showed him how to make pink by mixing red and white.

In the field, a cat found a patch
of flattened corn and went to sleep
in the sunshine.
"Now we need yellow, red, blue,
purple, green, white,
pink and..."

“BLACK,” said Patrick.

“Jet black,” agreed Aunt Emily.

A field mouse tiptoed out of its nest,
right past the sleepy, snoozy cat.
“Now we need yellow,
red, blue, purple,
green, white, pink,
black and...”

"GREY," said Patrick.

Aunt Emily showed him how to make grey by mixing black and white.

A sneaky fox slipped through the corn, its nose twitching. *Mmmm!* It could smell lots of nice, juicy things to eat.

"Now we need yellow, red, blue, purple, green, white, pink, black, grey and..."

"ORANGE," said Patrick.

Aunt Emily showed him how to make orange by mixing red and yellow.

Woof! Woof! Aunt Emily's dog woke up, eager to join in the fun!

"Easel, you naughty boy," cried Aunt Emily, as he chased all the animals away.
"Now we only need yellow," said Patrick, laughing.

"But look!" said Aunt Emily. "Maybe we need the other colours after all."

Yellow
Red
Blue
blue and red make purple
yellow and blue make green
white and red make pink
white and black make grey
yellow and red make orange
White
Black

MORE TITLES FROM FRANCES LINCOLN CHILDREN'S BOOKS

COLOURS
A First Art Book
Lucy Micklethwait

Red hat! Pink heart! Black bat!
Here are 18 brilliant works of art carefully chosen to illustrate a range of familiar colours.
Artists include Botticelli, Hiroshige, van Gogh and Peter Blake – something new on every page.
A perfect way to discover great art for the very young!

ISBN 978-1-84507-550-7

LEMONS ARE NOT RED
Laura Vaccaro Seeger

Lemons are not RED.
Lemons are YELLOW.
Apples are RED.
Introduce young children to the world of colour in this simple, original and utterly beguiling book.
As red lemons magically turn yellow, purple carrots turn orange, and white reindeer turn brown,
young readers will love guessing what could be next.

ISBN 978-1-84507-605-4

CAMILLE AND THE SUNFLOWERS
Laurence Anholt

One day, a strange man arrives in Camille's town. It is the artist, Vincent van Gogh.
His extraordinary paintings of the sunflowers and the Starry Night entrance the young boy.
But not everyone appreciates the genius of Camille's 'Sunflower Man' and Vincent is forced to leave the town.
Camille and the Sunflowers is a classic tale about acceptance of those who are different.

ISBN 978-0-7112-2156-7